First U.S. edition 2017

Library of Congress Catalog Card Number pending
ISBN 978-0-7636-9339-8

17 18 19 20 21 22 FGF 10 9 8 7 6 5 4 3 2 1

Printed in Shenzhen, Guangdong, China

This book was typeset in Goudy Infant.
The illustrations were done in gouache.

Nosy Crow
an imprint of
Candlewick Press
99 Dover Street
Somerville, Massachusetts 02144

www.nosycrow.com
www.candlewick.com

Pip and Posy
The New Friend

Axel Scheffler

An imprint of Candlewick Press

Pip and Posy were
going to the beach.

They unpacked their things.

"Don't forget to wear your hat, Pip," said Posy.

They collected shells.

They dug a little hole.

And they waded in the ocean.

While Posy was taking a nap,

Pip noticed a boy next to them.

"I'm Zac," said the boy.
"Would you like to play with me?"

"Yes, please!" said Pip.

Zac and Pip played with the beach ball

and did handstands.

Zac even let Pip try on
his goggles and flippers.

Pip and Zac were laughing so much
that they woke Posy up.

"Come and play with us, Posy!" said Pip.

But Posy didn't like Zac and Pip's games.

She felt left out.

When Zac said, "Let's get some ice cream,"

Posy went with them.

But then . . .

a sea gull stole Zac's ice cream!

Oh, dear!

Zac was **very** sad.

Poor Zac!

Then Posy gave Zac her last coin so he could buy himself another ice cream.

"Thank you, Posy," said Zac.

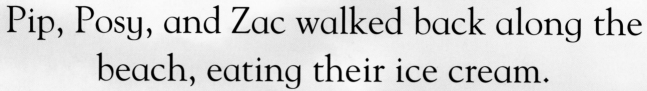

Pip, Posy, and Zac walked back along the
beach, eating their ice cream.

"What would you like
to do next, Posy?" said Pip.

Posy said, "Let's build a huge sand castle!"

So that's what they did.

Hooray!